Forward

The Entrusted Servant is a sensational tale of an enslaved prince and is a Romanian folk tale that reached the populace of Eastern Europe by word of mouth as have many other tales in Europe across the centuries. A similar example is Snow White.

The tales were mostly heard at the end of a long workday at the time when most family members were getting a chance to relax while tending to domestic activities such as repairing clothes, knitting, cleaning tools, preparing dinner, etc.

This particular tale was first published by Romanian author, Ion Creanga in the 19th Century. It has finally made it way out west for the rest of the world to enjoy.

Dr. Sorin Issvoran

Acknowledgements:

Kurt Snibbe, Pictorial Editor and Cover Design

I would like to dedicate this book to my parents as well as my children and grandchildren.
By translating this book into English, it is my hope that future generations will be delighted and inspired by the story within these pages.
Dr. Sorin Issvoran

The Tale of the Entrusted Servant

Once upon a time, there was a King whose older brother ruled as Emperor in a country far away from his own kingdom. The Emperor was known to his subjects as Emperor Green.

Emperor Green had only daughters and no sons to inherit his throne. Many years went by in which the King and the Emperor did not see each other, for their kingdoms were at opposite ends of the world. In the vast distance between the two kingdoms were many lands ravaged by wars and dangerous roads. Indeed, the few people who traveled such a great distance through such peril never returned to their homes again. So it was that as the Emperor's daughters and the King's sons grew older, they never met.

Emperor Green, though once young and valiant, began to feel his age. He feared that he was nearing death and was without any sons to rule his empire. He sent word to his younger brother through a trusted messenger, asking the King to send to him the bravest of his three sons to become Emperor after his death.

When the King received the message, without wasting a moment he declared, "My beloved sons, I just received a message from your Uncle, Emperor Green. He desires to give his empire to the bravest of you to rule over it. The land is prosperous and beautiful, but whoever inherits it must travel there on his own to prove that he is worthy. We must satisfy his last wish, both for my brother's sake and for the people of his kingdom."

The King's oldest son responded, "Father, I am owed this honor, since I am the oldest. Give me clothes and supplies for travel and bring me a noble horse and my finest armor so that I can prevail. I will leave before dawn breaks and you will have great pride that your son shall be Emperor!"

"All right, my eldest son. If you feel brave enough to go so far and face so many dangers to rule over my brother's nation, then get ready to leave. Choose a horse from my stable, take all the money and clothes you need and the armor that suits   you. May God watch over your way, my fair son!"

The young prince bid farewell to his brothers and father and kissed his hand with gratitude. The King gave him a written message for the Emperor. The Prince mounted on top of his horse and joyfully left for his uncle's empire.

The King was determined to see for himself if his son was truly worthy and went back to his quarters. He disguised himself with a bear pelt and rode on horseback through a secret, faster way across the plains, so that he could arrive ahead of his son at the bridge the King knew he would cross. He hid underneath it and waited.

The young prince soon arrived and once he was in sight of the bridge, he thought he saw a giant bear running toward him with a horrible, menacing growl.

The Prince's horse halted suddenly and reared on his hind legs, almost throwing him to the ground. When the young prince realized he could not master the horse, he reversed his course and returned home. His heart filled with dread as he thought of facing his father, but he felt he had no choice.

Taking the secret path, the King came back home ahead of his son. He hid his disguise and waited peacefully in his quarters. Finally, his son showed up, out of breath and agitated. He looked quite different from the confident man he had been on his departure.

"My son, you've returned so soon! Tell me, have you forgotten something?" the King asked with feigned astonishment. "You seem overwrought! What befell you on the road to my brother's empire?"

"I will tell you the truth, Father. I did not forget anything. When I arrived at the bridge, a horrible bear charged at me and I could go no farther out of fear. Having survived his claws and escaped with my life, I thought it wiser to return home to you, and not become prey to the wild beast. I dare not face such dangers again. If any of my brothers wishes to take my place, I will give him my blessing. As for me, I do not need to rule over any empire. I do not need to subject myself to such tortures and terror across the world just to satisfy my fancy to inherit something there, or any other place."

The King was troubled and his face grew dark. "You are right, my son. You do not have the fabric of an Emperor and an empire would not prosper under your rule. It is wiser for you to stay aside. Thank God that there is no shortage of frogs all around us, as long as water is abundant. I only despair at what will happen to my brother and his empire without a successor."

"Dearest Father," said the middle son, "I am ready to go, should you grant me your blessing!"

The King looked at him, doubtful. "You do have my blessing, yet I am afraid you will return in shame as your brother did. I foresee that you will meet some other adversity, some fierce animal to block your way! God alone can tell. But how can I refuse you? Go, then and try your luck. Perhaps you will catch it by the tail. Remember these old words of wisdom: The way you you prepare your bed determines your comfort, or lack of it when you go to sleep. Should you succeed, we will praise God in Heaven! If you do not, you shall not be the first to fail."

The middle son eagerly began preparations for his chance to prove himself to his father and brothers. He took along the King's message to Emperor Green. He bid goodbye to his two brothers and left in the early hours of the following morning.

He proceeded at a leisurely pace until the night's darkness fell all around him. Upon reaching the same bridge where his brother failed, he found himself face to face with a terrifying bear, who charged at him with a ferocious roar. The horse panicked and in its fear jumped and ran back so fast that the Prince could hardly hold on. So overwhelmed by the experience, he gave up the ambition of ruling in that far away country. He returned to his father, overcome with shame.

"You return to me in the same manner as your older brother. As the wise say: Save me from the ducklings, since I am not afraid of the dogs who chase the ducklings," The King said, his voice heavy with disappointment.

"How can you say such words to me, Father? Bears are more fearsome than ducklings and dogs. This bear was so enormous and vicious, it could tear to shreds an entire army. It is a miracle I am still alive. As for the empire, I could care less. Thank God, we have no shortage of food in our household."

At that second shame fell upon his family, the King grew very angry. "I was blessed with sons, but cursed as well, for not one is worthy of my brother's empire! You know the importance of this quest, but you cannot even summon the bravery to face an animal less than a day's ride from home. With such cowardice, you do not deserve the food you eat! You boast that you are the sons of a King, but have no more valor than a rat. My aging brother shall be waiting for his noble nephews until the earth's last day."

Hearing this, the youngest of the three sons turned redder in the face than the crest of a rooster. He hid in the garden outside the palace, where he wanted to cry in solitude over his father's harsh words. While he pondered, not quite knowing how to handle this humiliation, he suddenly noticed an old woman with a hunched back, leaning heavily toward the ground. She walked over to him.

"What makes you so sad, kind prince?" she asked. "Chase away the pain crushing your heart and take my counsel. You will face only good luck at every crossroad you reach from now on. You have no reason to grieve. Instead, look for some compassion in your heart for the old woman that I am and spare some coin for me."

"Please, leave me alone with my thoughts. I have enough worries of my own," the Prince

11

muttered.

"Young Prince!" she replied, "For it is God's will that you become Emperor! Share your worries with me. I may be able to help you."

Hardly listening, the youngest prince said, "Little mother, I beg you, do not torment me any further. I am already weary with troubles."

"Kind prince," she insisted again, "Do not spurn me so quickly. There is no way to predict from which direction your help will come!"

"Meaningless words. What help could an old woman give to a prince?"

"I may be an old woman, kind prince, but the Almighty God bestows His blessings on even the humblest of His creations. My back is bent to the ground and I am clothed in rags, but I am able to foresee the schemes of the most powerful rulers on this earth. Often I have laughed myself to tears at their helplessness and witless ways. I have seen so many things with these eyes over many centuries that weigh heavily on my frail shoulders! Little prince, if you had as much power as I do, you could cross lands and seas, play with our planet earth like a toy, make the human race turn on the tip of your fingers. Your whims could become the law of the land...so harken to this old, humpbacked woman! May God forgive me, I lost track of what I was trying to say! Kind Prince, show mercy to a poor, old beggar!"

The king's son was deeply shaken by her plea. He took the coin which he had in his pocket and looking at her with compassion, gave it to her.

"Here, little mother, take this. I can only give you this much. God will add to it what is still missing."

"May the Lord in Heaven reward you," replied the old woman with a grateful smile, "and may He grant you a long life, gentle prince, for I can see what awaits you. You will become Emperor. You will be the most loved and powerful ruler that this world has ever seen! And now, fair prince, let me also tell you one more thing: A good deed is never wasted. Look into my eyes and listen carefully to what I have to tell you.

"Go to your father and ask him to give you his horse, his armor and his wedding clothes. Listen closely, as this will be the only way you will succeed where your brothers have failed. Yes, the Almighty has chosen to grant you this honor. Know that your father will argue with you and will not want to let you go. You will have to beg him for his permission, but in the end, he will give it.

"The King's wedding clothes will be worn and tattered, his armor rusty, and his horse old and feeble. It will only come to you if you leave in the center of the stable   a tray containing burning, red-hot charcoal. The horse that approaches it is the horse who knows how to lead you on the road to your uncle's empire. This horse   will also save you from many grave dangers. Do not forget my words! We will meet again, in some remote corner of the earth. Even mountains face   each other in time, unlikely as it may seem to you at a first   glance. As for humans, they move and have far more reasons to meet again!"

As she spoke, a white shroud began to envelop her frail body and raise her into the air, carrying her to the clouds, then higher and higher until she was out of sight. The Prince was caught by a sudden chill, but whether it was from wonder or fear, he could not decide. He breathed deeply for a few moments as his calm returned and then his mind was made up. When he went before his father, it was with self-assurance.

"Father, give me the chance to travel to my uncle, Emperor Green," the youngest prince said boldly.

His father was astounded. "My little boy, I did not expect to hear such words coming out of your mouth," he said. "Your brothers abandoned their dignity and pride, and I had given up hope. You are the youngest and untested. Your brothers are far more experienced. What would happen if you encountered a vicious beast on the road? You, too, would turn home to save your own life and be humiliated."

The Prince shook his head. "Whether I succeed or fail, I promise you that I will not come back even if I meet Death itself on the road."

"Very well, if you have already made up

your mind to go, I cannot stop you. But believe me, my son, should you set out on this quest and return to me with it unfulfilled, you will find no place in my home." The King was loathe to see his youngest son fail as his older sons had, and hoped that his hard words would deter the Prince. But he saw the determination in his son's brow.

"Father, it is my duty to try. I do not depend on luck, but only my own bold heart and the will to bring honor to you and my uncle. What will be will be. Only God will determine the outcome. The only favor I ask from you, if I may, is to let me have your old horse, the armor and the clothes you wore when you were married. And then I will leave without delay."

At his son's strange request, the King was even more perplexed. "My poor old horse? Who is to tell where his bones are rotting? Who planted this senseless thought in your mind? Did they also say that you shall fly to the moon on the same horse?"

"Dear father, this is all I ask of you. Whether the horse is alive and where he is to be found shall be my problem. Only grant me your permission to take it as my own."

"You can have the horse, my child, if it still lives. And so shall I grant your other requests. May they help you to fulfill your promise."

With that, the young prince took off to find what the old woman had told him he must take. In the dusty corners of his father's armory, he found the wedding garb and armor, which was in poor condition and looked as ancient as Mother Earth. In that same forsaken place, he found an ancient sword. He wiped off the dust, polished the metal, and restored it to its former glory.

Afterward, he filled a tray with glowing hot charcoal and entered the stable where the horses were sheltered. He then placed the tray down on the floor, next to them. An old horse rushed immediately to the tray and swallowed a mouthful of charcoal. It looked fragile, ugly and unsteady on his legs. Shocked, the Prince hit the old horse on his head with the hot tray.

"Filthy old skeleton! You, of all horses in this shelter, had the nerve to come to me and eat the hot charcoal meant for my father's noble horse! Stay back or you will be sorry," he warned. The horse ate another lump of charcoal, and the Prince slapped it on the neck. The third time the horse leaned over the tray and swallowed the rest of what was left.

The Prince lost his temper and hit the horse as hard as he could. Exasperated, he asked himself, "Do I take this horse along, or should I turn him loose? People will laugh at me and I will be an embarrassment to the King. I would look far more dignified walking alone than with a feeble horse such as this."

While he deliberated with himself, the shabby old horse shook its back three times and suddenly its coat turned shiny and smooth like that of a young stallion. With a ripple of flesh, its legs and back were strong again. It was the most magnificent horse the Prince had ever seen.

The horse looked straight into the eyes of the Prince and talked to him with a human voice.

"Jump onto my back and hold on tightly, Prince!"

Mystified, the Prince did what he was told and the horse flew up into the air, carrying him into the clouds. They soon returned to the ground, with the speed of an arrow. As soon as his hoof brushed against the grass, the horse took off again and carried the Prince all the way to the moon and returned back at the speed of thunder! He then flew for a third time, reaching the sun, and swooped back to the earth even faster. As they touched the ground, the horse spoke again.

"Master, how do you feel about me now?

Did you ever expect to reach the sun with your toes, the moon with your hands or search through the clouds for the crown of your kingdom?"

"I have no sufficient words of praise, valued companion. I feared for my life and thought I might die of vertigo. You nearly killed me!"

"I felt just as crushed, Master, under your three lashes, which nearly killed me too! And now you have felt my pain. An eye for an eye and a tooth for a tooth! Now you have seen both sides of me. For now, I will change again as I was when you saw me first in the stable. I will keep you company everywhere you go. All you need to tell me is how fast you want me to carry you; like the wind, or perhaps as fast as the thoughts of your mind?"

"If you carry me at the speed of my thoughts, I will surely die. But if you carry me at the speed of the wind, you will do me well, my charming dear horse," replied the Prince.

"As you wish. Get on my saddle, and I will take you to wherever you want to go."

The Prince climbed on, and while

caressing the   horse's mane, he said, "Fly softly, my little horse."

The horse took the air and flew like the wind. They arrived back at the palace and the Prince went to bid farewell to his father.

"Welcome, brave son," said the King as his son walked into the throne room. "So this is the horse you chose! Whether it is my own of long ago, I cannot tell. May his old, brittle bones not break beneath you."

"I chose this horse as my companion and he will bear me well. It will be safer on the road if I do not draw attention to my presence. I will go as quickly as I can, on horseback or on foot."

With all his supplies ready, the Prince said goodbye to his father and kissed his hand. The King handed him the letter for Emperor Green and in the early evening he departed riding on his horse. He rode steadily until night fell.

By the time he reached the bridge, a bear jumped right into the middle of the road, growling and looking as if it was ready to crush the Prince with its giant paws. Yet the horse went on straight ahead with furious determination while the Prince, unshaken, raised his club to hit the bear. At that very instant, the Prince heard a shout that sounded quite human.

"Do not hit me, dear son of mine! It is I your father!"

The Prince dismounted, mouth agape. His

father let his disguise fall away and embraced his son.

"Son, you chose well your companion for the road. Whoever advised you gave wise counsel and you showed good judgment to follow it. It seems that you have indeed found my old horse who protected me in my younger years and now he will serve you. Do not delay your journey anymore. You have proved your worth to me. You will meet many on your journey. Some of them may be pure of heart, but many will aim to do you harm. Listen closely. Do not trust those with red hair. Trust them less than pestilence! And even worse than these people, you must not trust beardless men. These men are fully grown but have no hair on their face. Do not accept their help, or surely misfortune will fall upon you. Take along this bearskin. Who can tell? Perhaps you will have need of it."

The King patted the horse on the neck affectionately and wrapped both of them in his arms one last time, saying, "May peace be with you, my dear ones! Only God in Heaven can tell when we will see each other again."

The Prince climbed onto the saddle. The horse shook his body and turned into the young stallion that the King remembered from his younger days. Then, the horse and the Prince took off down the road. The King watched them disappear into the distance, praying that God would grant them a long life and that one day he would hear his son tell the story of his journey.

*   *   *

The Prince and his horse kept going for a day. Then, the day stretched into two more days and two more stretched into forty-nine days, until the road took them to a giant forest. They had barely penetrated this wilderness when out of nowhere a beardless man appeared before them.

" I am most delighted to meet you, valiant knight! This place is dangerous for anyone traveling alone. Wild beasts wait many long days for a lone traveler to wander into their paths. I know this area well and you would be wise to accept my help."

"Perhaps there are dangers ahead," replied the Prince, as he took a better look at the beardless stranger, searching deep into his eyes, "but I will continue on my own nonetheless." He pressed his boots lightly against the horse's sides and they went deeper into the forest.

Before long, they encountered the beardless fellow again, though he was in a disguise and they did not recognize him. He bent and strained his voice so that it sounded low and reassuring.

"May you be blessed with a good journey ahead of you, Sir!"

"Thank you, good fellow," the Prince replied. "May God bless you as well, with a generous and sincere heart."

"God would be merciful indeed if He blessed everyone with the kind of heart he gave me. What is the virtue of having a good heart? Everyone knows that brave people lack good luck! Listen to me young man, do not be angry at me if I say what I would say to my own brother. Ever since I was a child, I have always been placed amidst circumstances where I could be of service to strangers. Had I not enjoyed working, I would have suffered, because I was born to fulfill others needs. But I am cursed to run forever without being rewarded! I have always faced scoundrels who became my masters, and I fear that after long, I am bound to embody that old saying, 'When you serve scoundrels, you become one, yourself!' If only I could find myself a master to match my heart, I would take care of him the way I would treat the finest treasure! Are you in need of an escort, great sir? You seem to have well tailored pockets and you could make good use of my services. You are traveling through hazardous surroundings. Who can tell what may come up and the hardships you will face?"

"No, not now," the Prince barked, growing anxious, his fingers gripping his club tighter. "I will help myself."

The Prince galloped away, farther and farther in to the dark forest. He soon reached a place where all traces of trails vanished. Neither he nor his horse knew which way to go, and they trotted in circles with confusion.

"I can't believe it! Look at this jungle! How will I find my way out?" the Prince whispered to himself. Not a trace of a village in sight, no small inn, nothing at all. If he kept going, he knew he would end up even more lost. There was nothing ahead but wilderness. "I should have brought along that odd-looking creature, that second fellow I met a while ago. It is not his fault if he looks beardless like his mother! My father may have cautioned me to mistrust men unable to grow their own beards, but what else am I to do? It is bad enough to deal with bad matters and people, but there is also a good side too if you want to see it. If you cannot see the good, then the outcome may be even worse!"

While pondering what direction he should take, the beardless fellow appeared again. This time he was dressed differently and rode a magnificent young horse. Distorting his voice again with a superior tone of commiseration, he remarked, " Poor young fellow, the road you choose could hardly be worse! Clearly you are a stranger here, and lost. So lucky of you to have met me before you entered the ravine. You would have met your death in it! Take a look down there into that valley. There lives a mad bull. He is known to have killed a number of innocent travelers. Even I, tough as I am, I do not brag about it. I was very lucky the other day to only barely save myself from his grip.

You had better follow your way back where you came from. But should you continue on ahead, it would be wise to find an escort to show you the way. I myself could show you, in fact."

"I will take your offer of help, valiant man," replied the Prince. "But I will be forthright with you. My father discouraged me from trusting those who have red hair, and especially those who are naturally beardless. He told me not to deal with them, no matter what."

"Let me tell you, traveler, you would have wasted countless days looking for an escort to your liking in this land. All of the inhabitants in this area are beardless. That is how God made us. And why should that bother you? Have you not heard that ancient saying, 'No one rushes to get threads out of a rug which is about to fall apart'? The hunter who finds a shortage of larks, will also settle for blackbirds. Be glad you could find me. Hire me while I am here. Soon, you will not be able to do without me. I know my worth! I obey one law only: to serve my master with unwavering dedication! Do not ponder anymore. I fear the night will catch us still here."

"I have always taken my father's counsel, and dismissing it now gives me a strange feeling in my gut. But just today, I have met three beardless men, so I believe you when you say that I have arrived in a land where all grown men do not have beards. Therefore, good or bad, I must hire you to find my way through this wilderness." And so the odd-looking man led the Prince along the path.

They had only been walking a short while when the Prince's new companion complained of feeling thirsty, and asked for a drink of water from his flask. When the guide tasted the water, he drew back with a grimace of disgust on his face, and then emptied the water from flask on the ground. The Prince was stunned.

"Just what do you think you are doing? Did you not notice how hard it is to find water in this area? With   all this heat, we will die from thirst! You have doomed us!"

"Do not be angry, Master! Your water was stale and it would have made us sick to keep drinking it. But do not worry, soon enough we will arrive at a well with water that is pure, fresh and cold. We will stop there for a moment to rinse your flask and fill it before continuing our journey. Beyond that well, the water will be much scarcer."

They continued until they reached a clearance where they saw a well near a cluster of majestic oak trees. The well cap was lying on the ground next to it. The well was deep, and there was no wheel or lever to dip into it, only a stepladder for someone to descend inside to the level of the pool.

"Let us see, beardless escort, how worthy you are!" the Prince said.

The guide, with a wide and cunning smile on his face went down the ladder, deep inside the well. There, he filled the flask and attached it to his belt. While leaning down towards the pool, he called to the Prince.

"It feels so wonderful down here with the water nymphs around me at the edge of this fresh water pool. How I would love to remain down here. May the good Lord forgive all sins done by the man who dug this well. He offered

31

an excellent service to anyone coming this way. On a hot day such as this one, the fresh air inside this place is a treasure."

He stayed there a while longer. After returning to the surface he remarked, "Oh, how refreshed I feel! I almost feel as if I could grow wings and fly. You should come down here too for a short while! You will feel born again and so completely relaxed and light as a feather."

The young prince, still naive in so many ways, followed the advice of his beardless escort and entered the well, abandoning all worries about what could happen. While he brought handfuls of water up to his face, the beardless man suddenly covered the entrance of the well with the cap. All went dark inside. Then, he thrust himself on top of the lid and yelled while addressing the Prince with derision.

"Ha! I have finally lured you into my trap. You did not succeed to avoid the fate you feared! Now you are helpless. You must   tell me all about you,who you are, where you are coming from and where you are going. If you do not, here, is where your bones will rot!"

What was the Prince to do? He told him

everything, down to the last detail. What would a man not do to save his own life?

"And there is the truth of it, straight out of your mouth, you filthy viper," said Beardless. "If you lied to me, you will regret it. Even now I could still get rid of you. Nothing could stop me, but I could use a young and able man to serve me. If you want to see sunlight and green pastures again, you must swear to me on your sword that you will obey me without question or hesitation, and that you will submit to me in every way, even if I will order you to throw yourself into a pit of fire. From now on, I will be the nephew of Emperor Green and you will be my servant. You will remain no more than my servant until you die and even after your resurrection. Should you divulge a single word about what happened here, that will be the end of you. If you consent to live in submission to me, I will spare you. Give your answer now in plain words."

The Prince realized he was now a helpless victim in the grips of Beardless, who came to take advantage of him during his moment of distress. There was nothing he could do. He swore unconditional obedience and good faith to Beardless. He gave up his money, armor and all he had. Only then was he finally dragged out of the well. But the Prince was given back his sword and requested to kiss it in order to consecrate his commitment to his enemy.

"From now on your name shall be 'Entrusted Servant'," Beardless declared. "and you will have no other!"

With that, they both got on their horses. Beardless, now the new master, walked in front and the Entrusted Servant followed behind him.

The two rode day in and day out, crossing nine different seas and nine different countries on different continents and at last, they finally reached the great empire ruled by Emperor Green. Upon their arrival, Beardless introduced himself to the Emperor, handing the message from the King. Once he read it, the Emperor was overjoyed that his nephew was able to come so far and through so much danger and he wasted no time in introducing him to the Court and to his daughters, the young princesses. They received him with all the honors due to the son of a king and the anticipated successor to the throne.

Beardless took the Entrusted Servant aside and said in a threatening voice, "Remain out of sight, inside the animal shelter, taking good care of my horse. Treat him as carefully as you would your own eyes. If I go there and find that you did a poor job, I will have you cooked in the oven!"

"Yes, Master," replied the Entrusted Servant, lowering his eyes in submission. He ran back to stable, as ordered.

The princesses, who happened to witness this scene, felt sorry for the Entrusted Servant and his undeserved humiliation, then pleaded with the Beardless in soft tones.

"Cousin, it is unfair to treat him this way. If God blessed us at birth with the privilege to be masters, we should offer sympathy and understanding toward our subjects. They too, are human beings like us."

"Come now, my dear cousins," replied Beardless, displaying his natural perfidy, "you are not acquainted enough with the realities of life. If animals were not domesticated by men, they would have chewed down most humans to the bone long ago. And most human beings are also animals who need to be disciplined in order for others to flourish. If not, we will face doom. May God guard us from all beggars who act like kings!"

From that time forward, the young ladies, who ordinarily spoke with each other about trivial things, began talking about the unseemly behavior of Beardless. They could not put his ugliness out of their minds and could not swallow his justification. Even though they believed that he was their blood, they found it hard to see past his manner. The old words of wisdom haunted their thoughts, "You never get good bread using bad grain".

From that time on, they began whispering to each other that Beardless was not like them in mind or body. They also felt that somehow, his serving slave, whom he called Entrusted Servant, had a good heart. Deep down, the connection they felt to the Entrusted Servant made them suspect the truth of it all, that Beardless was not their real cousin. They began to find it difficult to feign happiness at his presence and even wanted to disown him, though they worried about angering Emperor Green.

Shortly after, Beardless dined with his proclaimed uncle, cousins and the Court. A server brought dishes from the palace kitchen and at last he brought a fresh salad that was remarkably delicious.

The Emperor commented, looking at Beardless, "Tell me, nephew, have you ever tasted a salad so exquisite as the one you are eating now?"

"Never, Uncle! I was about to ask you where you found such marvel. It is exceptional. I could eat a roomful and still not have enough of it!"

"It is indeed a marvel and you could never imagine how difficult it is to find. This special leaf grows only in the Bear's garden. There are very few people who succeed in reaching that place and fewer still who come back alive. Only one woodsman in my whole empire knows how to get inside. He brings back some of it every now and then and gives it to me."

When Beardless heard this, he thought of a clever plot to rid himself of the Entrusted Servant and the risk he posed.

"Uncle, let me tell you, I would be stunned if my servant would be unable to get it, even if it were to grow in the heart of the desert."

The Emperor gave a barking laugh. "You underestimate the danger of these lands if you assume that a fellow like him, unacquainted with those surroundings, could achieve such an exceptional task. Perhaps you tire of your servant and want to get rid of him!"

"Not at all, Uncle! Do not be so concerned. I am willing to bet he will bring us the same leaf and in ample supply. I am proud to offer up this favor in your honor. I know how capable he is!"

Beardless called for the Entrusted Servant and ordered him with an authoritative voice, "Leave immediately and bring to the Emperor the leaves you see on this table as a gift. You will find it in the Bear's garden. Make haste! I warn you, if you dare disobey me, I will be after you and find you even if you hide in a mouse hole!"

The Entrusted Servant returned to the stable and headed straight to his horse. He caressed his companion and spoke sadly. "My gentle horse, if only you could guess what misfortune lays ahead of me! May God bless my father, who advised me wisely before I left home. I did not pay enough attention to his advice, and now, here I am, forced to obey this aging monkey's every whim. It is of my own doing!"

"Master," replied the horse, "from here on, it does not matter whether it was ignorance or misfortune that brought the knife to the victim's throat. We cannot change what is past. Be brave! Jump on my back and let's go. I happen to know where we must go, and God willing, we will manage once more."

The Entrusted Servant, comforted by his friendly horse, recovered his courage and jumped onto the saddle. At first, the horse trotted like all horses so, following a trail on the ground. But when they were out of sight of the castle, it transformed into the gallant, strong, youthful creature.

"Master, hold tight to the saddle," the horse said. "We will fly fast like the wind, all across the earth. Remember, the Devil may be clever, but only God is almighty. Do not lose faith, we will have the last word with this Beardless, it is still not too late!"

The horse flew up to the heavens, carrying the Entrusted Servant through the clouds and after sometime, they returned back to the earth. This voyage carried them over forests, mountains, the crests of the waves of many seas and oceans and then they landed quite softly on an island. The horse touched ground near a small, secluded cottage. The soil was covered with thick moss, supple like satin and brilliant green.

Here, the Entrusted Servant finally set foot on the ground. He looked ahead toward the cottage and gasped, for the old beggar to whom he offered a coin emerged from within. She came out to greet him.

"Well, Entrusted Servant, I was right, was I not, when I told you, ' Even mountains face each other in time. As for us humans, it is much easier', I am called Holy Mother Sunday. I know what troubles you have encountered since our last meeting. Beardless wants to get rid of you at all costs and for that reason, he sent you pick leaves from the Bear's garden. But do not worry! I know what you must do to survive this task. Stay here for the night and rest. Beardless will chew his fingers some day for all he is trying to do to you!"

The Entrusted Servant did not wait to be invited again. He thanked Mother Sunday for her hospitality, her kindness and the help she promised him.

"It is not I, but your generosity to the poor and your good heart that has rescued you in these trials," replied Mother Sunday as she turned to leave. "Go inside the cottage and take some reprieve from your struggles."

Mother Sunday left the place, walking barefoot over the moist grass to the back of the cottage, where she picked an armful of blooming poppies. She placed them in a large pot and boiled them in milk and honey, until it became a thick soup. She hurried fast to carry the soup to the Bear's garden not far from her home. Once there, she   poured the mixture inside the Bear's drinking well.

As she slipped away, she saw the Bear approach the   well. The beast was terrifying, spitting fire from its mouth, growling with a deafening force that could send chills down the spine of the bravest knight.

Once the Bear reached the well, it drank with great thirst and did not stop for some time. It licked its lips with delight. The water was sweet and delicious with all that Mother Sunday had added to it.

After it stopped drinking, the Bear began growling again, until it had exhausted all its energy. It dropped down to the ground heavily, sinking into a sleep so deep, the great beast looked dead. Even if a tree fell upon it, it would not have stirred. Mother Sunday returned back to her home as fast as she could and woke up the Entrusted Servant in the middle of the night.

"Take along the bearskin given to you by your father before your departure and go quickly! Follow the trail, climb over the fence and pick the leaves to bring back to the

Emperor. The Bear sleeps for now, but if it wakes up and attacks you, throw in its face the bearskin and run back to me as fast as you can!"

The Entrusted Servant followed faithfully the instructions given to him by Mother Sunday. Once in the garden, he collected a large pile of all the beautiful leaves he could pick into a bag and got ready to leave.

But at that very moment, the Bear awakened and charged after the Entrusted Servant. The Entrusted Servant threw the bearskin at it, blinding and confusing it and ran as fast as he could with the bag of leaves over his shoulder.

When he reached the cottage again, he thanked Mother Sunday for saving his life and helping him complete his task. He humbly kissed her hand and made his journey home, taking great care with the precious leaves.

*   *   *

The Entrusted Servant and his horse managed to get back to Emperor Green's palace after a long and challenging road back. He delivered the rare leaves to Beardless immediately.

The Emperor and his daughters watched in amazement. Beardless looked at the Emperor and said with a superior expression on his face.

"Well, Uncle, what have I told you?"

"What can I say? If I had such a man in my service, I would greet him most humbly," the Emperor said.

"Why do you think my father had him serve me, if not for his merits? I would not have complicated my life with him, if he did not have such abilities!"

Shortly after the Entrusted Servant's return, the Emperor showed to Beardless, with great pride, some enchantingly beautiful diamonds.

"Nephew," Emperor Green began, "did you ever see such unusual stones, so enormous and sparkling so brilliantly?"

"Uncle, I must confess, I have never seen any as magnificent as these, though I have seen many great jewels in my lifetime. Where did you find such beautiful stones?"

"Diamonds of this quality have only one source, the Stag. This Stag is unlike any other, studded with diamonds of a size even larger than these here. But that is not all. In the middle of the jewels upon his forehead is a diamond that shines as brilliantly as the sun! But the Stag is protected by some mysterious power, and if it should simply look at you with its eyes, you will drop dead instantly! For that reason alone, people do not dare to go near it. It is rumored that there are countless people and animals laying dead in that forest, felled by a single glance. No doubt, the Stag is bewitched, fed with dragon milk, or the Devil may tell what else, to make it so deadly. Perhaps it was made so by someone even worse than the Devil, for there are also some people even more wicked than the Devil himself--people who could be deterred by nothing, in spite all they have suffered. These people still try to capture the magic stag while it rests in its cave. Once in a great while, a fortunate soul wandering through that land finds a diamond that has fallen from the Stag's fur, whether from shaking or scratching. But this occurs no more than once in seven years! For a hunter, to find a stone like that brings riches to last a lifetime.

"When a hunter comes to the palace and brings such a diamond," continued the Emperor, "I pay him ten times the price he asks. Even so, I feel privileged to have acquired such a stone! Let me tell you, Nephew, these particular stones, are the greatest ever seen in my entire empire. There is no other place in the world where one can find diamonds of such purity and size! They have become famous far and wide, and many emperors and princes visit who visit want nothing more than take a look at these precious stones!"

"Good God," gasped Beardless, "Uncle, forgive me, but if that is so, then you are surrounded by cowards in this country. I bet you that my servant can bring you back the whole hide of this magical stag, including his head with all the diamonds upon it!"

Without waiting a moment, Beardless ordered that the Entrusted Servant be brought out to him and the Emperor at the table.

"Get ready to leave for the Forest of the

Stag," he told the Entrusted Servant. "You must find it on your own, and bring back the hide of the Stag, along with its head and all the precious stones upon it. If you fail, it shall be the end of you. Now, go! You have no time to waste."

The Entrusted Servant realized that he faced another impossible task that might destroy him. He mourned the fate that led him to be at the mercy of Beardless. Without a moment to rest, he went back to the stable and his faithful horse. He fondly caressed his companion with sadness and worry, then explained his new task.

"Should I prevail this time," he finished, " perhaps destiny wants me to continue living. Truthfully, my chances are very slim!"

"Regain your peace of mind, master!" replied the horse. "Every time you face dire times, you should respond with calm. After all, Beardless did not ask you to remove the millstone from a watermill and bring it back to the palace, did he?"

"But gentle horse, don't you see? What he is asking is much more challenging," replied the Entrusted Servant.

"Let me tell you something, the only thing we must do is get started on our way. The rest will be a child's game, you will see," said the horse confidently. "Do not be afraid, because I am familiar with the dirty tricks of Beardless. If I had the power, I would have given him what he deserves a long time ago. But let him expose his real, vile character a little longer. Believe me, these kinds of creatures belong to this world too, if for no other reason than helping us to grow wiser. Appease your thoughts by telling yourself that you, perhaps, are paying for some sins you have committed, and if not your sins, then your forefathers'. Remember the old saying, "Sometimes, when parents eat sour grapes, their children inherit weak teeth". Come now, don't lose yourself to dark thoughts! Mount the saddle and have faith in God, because His power is limitless. God will treat you, and me, with mercy in the days ahead. Don't you know that every- body's faith is already written in the book of destiny? God will help us and one day in the future, our misfortunes will come to an end!"

The Entrusted Servant was encouraged by

his horse's words and together they departed.

"Master, hold tight now! I will fly up to the sky, going through the thin blue air, above forests, over mountains, through fog, above hills and endless oceans. I will be looking for the Queen of the Fairies, wonder of beauty, who lives on her enchanted island."

When they were out of sight of the palace, the horse released his inner energy and took off into the sky. He flew towards the heavens, carrying along the Entrusted Servant. The horse was also a poet and he described their voyage, saying,

We will fly
Up into the sky
Through thin atmosphere
Without any fear!

When they found the island, the Queen saw them coming and she ran to them.

"Well, Entrusted Servant," she said in a soft voice, "you may not recognize me, but you know me and it looks like you need me again!"

"Yes, Mother Sunday I do," replied the

Entrusted Servant. "He looked very worried, pale with fear. "Beardless will not stop this madness until I am dead. If only I could die sooner then my suffering would be over! I would rather die a thousand times over than live a life like this!"

"Take heart, Entrusted Servant," said Mother Sunday, "You are braver than that! Gather your courage soon or I shall start thinking that you are ready to give up even faster than an old beggar woman would! Rest here tonight and I will find out a way to help you. God is supreme and He will not bless Beardless and his schemes! Be patient for you have come this far. You will not have to endure much more, but it is not over yet. You will face more requests like this one, as long as Beardless remains your master. But it is written in your destiny that you will survive and also that you will have the final word!"

"I believe you, Mother Sunday. And I am sorry that I despaired. I am merely overcome with the troubles that have fallen upon me," replied the Entrusted Servant.

"It is God's will," answered Mother

Sunday. "You cannot help it! Man tries the best he can, but God decides. One day your turn will come and from that time on, you will become great and powerful. With these hardships, you will grow wise, discerning and you will strive to be merciful to those who are unhappy or oppressed, because you will have known suffering. Until you get there, be patient, Entrusted Servant! That is the only way to defeat Beardless."

The Entrusted Servant had no words to respond, but he felt grateful to God for everything that happened to him both good and bad.

"If misfortune falls upon you again, do as I say. If it appears ahead of you, try to drag yourself behind it. If it follows you from behind, do not rush ahead. Instead, wait for it to reach you. This is the only way the world can go on. No one can change adversity, but you can give it a good shake! Now, let us discover a way to deal with the Stag, lest Beardless become impatient, whose every point of a finger and shift of the eye you are bound to obey," Mother Sunday said. She retrieved the glasses and the sword that once belonged to the Long Bearded Midget (but that is another story for another time). She handed the items to the Entrusted Servant, saying, "Take these. You will need them where you are going. God willing, we will finish this task soon."

They waited for the first song of the rooster early in the morning. Then they departed and headed for the forest where the Stag lived.

Once they arrived, they dug a trench deep enough to conceal them while they were standing. The trench was next to a pool with spring water, where the Stag came every day at about noontime to drink, and afterward stretch out on the grass and take a nap like a King until sunset. Upon awakening, it would leave and and not return until next day, always at the same hour.

"Entrusted Servant, get inside the trench and hide there for the rest of the day. Hold your sword tight in your hand. At noontime, after the Stag finishes drinking from the pool, it will lie down and will sleep with its eyes wide open. When you hear it snore, cut off its head with one stroke, then   jump back inside the trench. Do not leave the trench until sunset, for until that moment, the Stag's head will continue to call you by your name.   The Stag has one poisoned eye, and if he sets that eye on you, you will be finished! After the sun goes down, the Stag will finally be dead. Only then you can   leave your trench without fear. Remove its skin and head, and when you have done so,   come back and find me."

Mother Sunday returned   alone to her home. The Entrusted Servant remained hidden in the trench. At noon, he heard the Stag rustling through the high grass, coming to the pool. It burbled and drank, then burbled again and continued to drink until it could no   more. Then it began scraping the dirt, raising a cloud of dust in the air above him before laying down on the ground. There, he fell into a deep sleep and began snoring.

The snore was loud enough to rattle all of the surrounding leaves and twigs. As soon as the Entrusted Servant heard the snore, he came carefully out of his trench and severed its head off with one sharp blow from his sword cleanly in the middle of the neck. Then he jumped back into the trench as fast as he could. The Stag's blood started to gush out from all sides in a torrent. It flooded the trench, nearly drowning the Entrusted Servant. The Stag's head was struggling, overcome with pain and kept crying out loud.

"Entrusted Servant, Entrusted Servant! I heard about you many times before, but I have never seen you! Please come out for just one instant, so that I can take a look at you, and realize that you deserve this treasure, which I will trust in your hands! Then, my friend, I will die peacefully!"

But the Entrusted Servant stayed motionless. Inside the pit, the mass of clotting blood nearly as high as the trench almost suffocated him and his feet were stuck together so strongly he could not budge.

The head kept lamenting for some time. The Entrusted Servant remained silent and out of sight. Then finally, a deep silence fell upon the forest and he saw the colors of sunset! The Entrusted Servant finally emerged from his trench, skinned the Stag with utmost care and set it aside taking care not to dislodge any precious stones. Then he picked up the head of the Stag and returned to Mother Sunday.

"We have prevailed again!" Mother Sunday exclaimed.

"We have! It was with God's will and your help and counsel! All of this was done to please Beardless! If only destiny would make it possible that I regain my freedom from my master before my head becomes a skull...and even then, I will still feel that I endured more than a man may tolerate without losing his mind!"

"Leave him in God's hands, Entrusted Servant! Some day he will face his own master! Rest assured, he will get what he deserves. But now, you must leave and return the jewels to him. He will discover soon enough what destiny has in store for him!"

The Entrusted Servant thanked again kind Mother Sunday and humbly kissed her hand then returned the way they came.

*   *   *

As the Entrusted Servant and his horse made their journey back, large crowds gathered to see them and marvel at the sight of the large diamond shining in the middle of the Stag's head. It shined so intensely that Entrusted Servant seemed to carry along the sun itself as a trophy. Many kings and emperors came to meet him. Some were willing to offer him countless riches in exchange for the gems and others offered their daughters in marriage and in addition, half of their empires! He refused these offers with dignity and returned to his master.

On the enchanting evening of the Entrusted Servant's homecoming, Beardless lingered next to the Emperor and entertained the princesses. While admiring the view from the top of a tower, they noticed in the distance a bundle of sun rays scintillating and getting gradually closer. The closer they got, the more the sparkle blinded everyone.

A large crowd gathered to witness the wonderful sight. The Entrusted Servant came down the road to the palace carrying with him the pride of the Stag. He stopped in front of

Beardless and gave him the prize. The crowd fell silent.

Beardless retained his composure and told the Emperor, "Well, Uncle, how do you feel about this matter, now? You see that I was right."

"What can I say, Nephew," replied the Emperor, overwhelmed. "If I had a servant of such ability and devotion as yours, I would invite him to sit next to me at this table! He is worth his weight in gold!"

"I may express a word of regret at his burial," Beardless said, unable to hide the ugliness in his voice, "but I would never go beyond that, even if he were twice as good! He is not my mother's brother, to deserve such honor! A servant will always remain a servant, and his master will always remain his master! My servant has talents, but let me tell you, you have no idea what kind of devil this servant is within. He has given me countless troubles in the past and I happen to be the only one who knows how to handle him. In yesteryears, there was a saying, 'In an orchard, only fear establishes order'! Don't let yourself be fooled,

Uncle! I have seen that you are too kind with your subjects. That is why stags do not give you diamonds and bears keep you from their gardens. As for me, let me tell you that no one has been born yet who would dare throw rocks into my garden! If anyone would defy my will, I would tighten the rope around his neck until he gave in! Should God counsel you to retire and concede me your position at an earlier time than you planned, you will have a chance to see how I will transform your empire. The administrators will not drag their feet as they do now! There is no doubt in my mind that when you were younger, your empire was better, but now, you are declining, and your empire along with you."

Beardless went on and on, ranting like a crow and again repeated all he said before, until he exhausted the Emperor and princesses to the point that he forgot all about the Entrusted Servant, the Stag and everything else! The princesses eyed Beardless like the way a dog looks at a cat. Their hearts warned them that Beardless was a man lacking faith and any sense of justice. But they felt helpless, for they knew how desperately their father required an heir for the empire. So Beardless, even with all his malice, still had a future with an open horizon.

A few days later, Emperor Green gave a most elegant reception to honor his nephew. He invited illustrious guests, kings, princes, leaders, military dignitaries, nobility from the courts as well as lords from the countryside. When the festivities took place, the princesses ran to see Beardless and begged him to allow the Entrusted Servant to join the other servants at the table.

Beardless did not oppose them. He called the Entrusted Servant and gave him permission to stay there, on the condition that he remains at all times behind his master, while dinner was served. He told him that he must keep his eyes lowered and never look at the guests! Pointing at his servant with the sword he made him swear on long ago, he hissed, "If I find you insubordinate, I will cut your unworthy head off with one stroke and let it fly up in the air and down to the ground!"

"Yes, Master," the Entrusted Servant replied humbly. "I fully submit myself to your orders."

While the guests tasted the finest vintages set on the table, they began to notice a wonderful bird knocking at the window. The bird spoke with the voice of a young woman.

"Listen to me, you who drink and celebrate! Don't give one thought to the daughter of Emperor Red!"

The guests were shocked and stopped their merrymaking. Some whispered that Emperor Red was said to have the heart of a wild animal and that he never found enough human blood to drink. Others murmured that Emperor Red's daughter was an abominable witch and that she was known to demand human sacrifices.

Many of the guests hurried to confirm the rumors and said that the bird knocking with the beak against the window was the princess herself! She must have come from her palace, a long trip indeed, with the sole intention to provoke the guests into talking about her. Some worried that the bird was a spy and some simply spat on the floor to reverse any curses the princess may have been casting upon them.

The daughter of Emperor Red became the object of such extravagant gossip that it was impossible to figure out the truth of the matter. Beardless listened to everyone's mutterings, then suddenly stood and, with a supreme look on his face, he declared, "Nothing is worse than dealing with men who are scared of their own shadow! Honorable guests, are all of you innocent young shepherds who unable to make sense of what you have just heard!'

Beardless glimpsed what he thought was a smile upon the Entrusted Servant's face and grew wrathful. "Now I see what goes through your mind! Traitor, pretending to work for me! You know what goes on here, yet you do not say a word! Leave, right now and bring me the daughter of Emperor Red! Find her wherever she may be! Do it swiftly, or I will cut your head off!"

His spirit broken, the Entrusted Servant returned to stables once more.

"Here we are again, my friend. Beardless charged me to bring back to him the daughter of Emperor Red. No one knows where she is, but I must find her myself. It is as the folk say, 'When you get invited to a feast, you must eat what is offered on the table.' It looks like I have reached the end of my days in this world! Who is to tell what I must face now? The only thing one can say for sure is that the Devil must be involved and determined to persecute me. May God forgive me if I am wrong, but it seems to me that my mother brought me to life in this world under the protection of a bad star! I was once a prince, and yet I have grown accustomed to this degraded life. Heavenly Father, please spare this fellow man of all he has had to endure!"

"Master," said the horse, neighing emphatically, "Do not lament your fate! Remind yourself that, after the rain, the good weather returns every time. If men gave up their lives at every hardship, one would see only dead people alongside the roads! Have patience. Perhaps fate will smile at you in the end. Our obligation is to fight through adversity with hope. As folk often say, 'Given the luck, one can walk on fire and blood!' Now, regarding Emperor Red and where to find him, leave that up to me, Master. I will take you there. I visited his empire with your father when he was young. Come, get on my back and hold tight to the saddle. This time, I will reveal my power for Beardless to see, and enrage and poison his heart!"

They soared into the clouds and beyond, bathed by the sunrays and later in the moonlight, on and on in the direction of the domain of Emperor Red.

Back in the palace dining room, Beardless was overcome with rage. "How could I have been such a fool to not realize with whom I was dealing?" he thought. "I should have exterminated him long ago! If he does not perish on this journey, I will make sure to kill him. My sword will have the last say!"

"Now you finally see, Your Grace, and illustrious guests," Beardless said loudly."What could happen to any one of you if you feed a demon in good faith. The Entrusted Servant has shown his traitor's heart and has fooled me completely! It is well known that the Devil launches his most violent assaults against the towers which are tallest!" Everyone in the palace was stunned, as Beardless kept mumbling to himself all the hatred he felt for his slave, obsessed with what might happen to him.

All the while, the Entrusted Servant ventured on his horse through wild, solitary lands. He arrived at a bridge and prepared to cross it, when he noticed a crowd of ants going in the same direction to attend a wedding. He stopped for a while to ponder over the situation.

"If I take a single step, I will crush them by the thousands!" he thought. "It is better to go swim and risk drowning, than to risk crushing these ants."

With faith in God, he plunged into the stream, next to his horse and reached the far shore. Soon they were back on solid ground, continuing their journey, drenched to the bone and shivering.

Suddenly a flying ant came their way and said in a small voice they could hardly hear, "Entrusted Servant, I have heard of you and since you spared our lives on the bridge, and because you were so mindful not to spoil our joy, I want to offer you a service. Take along with you this wing! If you should need me, burn the wing and I will come to help you, together with our ant nation!" The Entrusted Servant took the tiny wing with great care, thanked the ant and continued on.

They rode for a while longer, until they heard a rumbling sound in the distance. It grew louder and louder. He looked right and saw nothing. Then he looked left and again saw nothing. He looked skyward and up above was a swarm of bees whirling above his head. They were soon all around him, buzzing with panic, unable to find a shelter where they could settle down.

The Entrusted Servant felt sorry for them, so he removed his hat and laid it on the grass.

Then he moved farther back while the bees discovered it with great relief, rushing inside his hat to rest.

The Entrusted Servant was joyful, for he always felt compassion for the creatures of the earth. He rushed right and left, in search of a stump that was halfway rotten. When he found one, he hollowed it out and padded the inside with small twigs rubbed with scented plants that he knew the bees loved. When he had completed the improvised beehive, he carried it on his shoulders to the spot where he left the bees. Then he removed them gently from his hat, transferring them inside the stump. He carried the stump to a quiet place and covered it with leaves to shelter the bees from sunlight and rain. The spot he chose was at the edge of a field which was covered with wild flowers. Only then did he return to the road to continue his quest.

He had just started upon the trail again when the Queen of the Bees flew up to him.

"Entrusted Servant, you have been so good to us and you did not have to do it. You have given us a home. I wish to return your favor. Please, accept this bee wing from me and save it! Should you ever need me, burn the wing and I will come to your aid."

The Entrusted Servant took the bee wing, wrapped it with great care and placed it in his pocket. He thanked the Queen of the Bees cheerfully, and departed.

Down the road, they entered a forest, where the Entrusted Servant noticed a giant man shaking with cold, trying to warm himself up next to an incredibly large fire made of twenty-four bundles of firewood. In spite of the impressive blaze, he was yelling at the top of his lungs about how he felt frozen to death.

The man was a shock to anyone who looked at him. He had terrible long ears that hung down low and thick, droopy lips. When he blew through them, the upper lip curled upwards into his cheeks while the lower dangled down to his belly. To make matters worse, frost erupted upon anything his breath touched and no one could get near him because his shivering sent tremors into the earth. Everything around him suffered with him. The wind groaned like a madman, the trees in the forest were a chorus of haunting laments, their branches covered in ice, the rocks screeched against each other and even logs in the fire sputtered and coughed violently. All the woodland creatures shrunk away from the frost inside their holes, shedding icy tears and cursing the moment they were born.

The hellish sight caused the Entrusted Servant to stop in his tracks and as soon as he did, he felt icicles forming on his face, around his nose, eyes and lips. The whole affair was so absurd and bizarre that he laughed aloud.

"The longer one lives, the stranger the things his eyes behold!" the Entrusted Servant shouted. "You, old devil, without lying to me, tell me for my peace of mind. Do you happen to be the Spirit of Winter itself? Surely you must be, for you are even freezing the great fire at your feet!"

"Enjoy your laughter, Entrusted Servant. Have your fun!" replied Frosty, while he kept shaking with cold. "Yet where you plan to go, you will not be able to succeed without me!"

"Then why don't you come along, if you are willing?" said the Entrusted Servant. "Besides, as you walk, you will warm up! It will not help you to stay in one place."

Frosty agreed and they left together. They walked for some time through that wilderness without trouble. But then, they reached a place where the Entrusted Servant noticed another man of giant proportions. This one looked even more strange than Frosty and walked behind twenty-four carts driven by oxen. As he walked, he swallowed voraciously the soil from the tracks left by the carts, and kept screaming how desperately hungry he felt, saying he would die of starvation.

"This is so ludicrous, I can hardly help but laugh!" said the Entrusted Servant. "What else is left to be seen in this world after this? That fellow must be the one who is called 'Hungry,' without any doubt! He is also called Famine, Cracked Bag and perhaps other names, because of his peculiar nature. The whole planet would not suffice to satisfy his hunger!"

"Entrusted Servant, you can keep laughing as much as you want! Yet you don't know one thing: where ever you plan to go you will not achieve anything without me!" said Hungry.

"If so, then join us!" said the Entrusted Servant. "As long as you do not expect me to carry you on my back!"

Hungry came along, following behind the Entrusted Servant and Frosty and together they continued the journey. After walking for another two and a half miles, they met another odd character. A tall, skinny young man was busy drinking huge amounts of water. He had emptied twenty-four ponds and also an entire river so big that it served five hundred water mills built on its shores. And still, this odd fellow kept groaning that he was dying of thirst.

"I cannot believe my eyes! This strange man will not appease his thirst, even after draining all the springs on this earth! This fellow can be no other than Thirsty, the son of Mother Draught!"

"You laugh at me, Entrusted Servant! Keep laughing," croaked Thirsty. As he spoke, water streamed out of his nostrils and ears like waterfalls. "But I tell you now, wherever you go, your journey is worthless without me!"

"Then you, too, must come with us," declared the Entrusted Servant. "The frogs will have no reason to curse you anymore and the water mills will be able to function again. May God forgive me for saying it, but I also think that if you go on like that, you will end up growing toads in your stomach!"

Thirsty followed along with the other odd members of the new group, behind the Entrusted Servant. The four of them wasted no time, knowing they had a long way to go.

Days later, in the morning, the Entrusted Servant spotted again something unusual and quite intriguing. He spotted a very large creature, shaped like a human being, but with only one eye. Even more peculiar was that, when he opened the eye, he couldn't see anything around him and would stumble like a blind man. Yet, when he closed his eye in daylight, or even at night, he could see everything perfectly, down to the inner core of the earth. He kept yelling loudly, "I see all and everything as if they are transparent! Above my head I see what no other eye is able to see, and when I look ahead of me, I see the sun on the other side of these hills, ready to set! I also see the moon and the stars falling into the sea. I see the treetops looking downward, animals with their legs facing upwards, and people with the heads pushing down on their shoulders! I see what nobody bothers to notice, like this wide open mouth facing me, unable to understand what goes on here."

"You would be better off if you could see yourself and admire what you look like!" called the Entrusted Servant. "May God save us from this absurdity! Anyone who sees this poor creature should take pity on him. No doubt, it was God's will for him to be this way. This fellow must be Big Eye Clairy! There is no other person on earth like him, one who sees all and notices everything, yet one incapable of seeing his own charming character. May God save him from anyone who would speak against him."

"Ridicule me until the day of the last judgment!" said the odd fellow. "But I say to you--where you are going, you will face much trouble if I am not around! The daughter of Emperor Red cannot be taken so easily. You may reach the Emperor and ask him to let you bring his daughter with you, but you will fail, unless I assist you."

"Come along, friend, if you'd like," said the Entrusted Servant. "We are a strange company and you are welcome to follow us."

So Big Eye Clairy joined the team as well, and the five of them continued the long journey toward the country of Emperor Red. This time, they hardly walked for two hours before encountering another strange being. It was a most disgusting looking young fellow, holding a bow and arrow and hunting for birds.

Archery was not his only talent. He was able to elongate his body so far that even the Devil could fathom his length. He could also stretch at will from his sides and wrap the whole earth in his arms, or reach to touch the moon, stars and sun with his hands. He could make himself as tall as he wanted and if his arrows missed their mark, it made no difference to him. He would stretch up and catch the bird in flight! Then he would twist the bird's neck and joyfully eat it, feathers and all. At that moment, he had in front of him a large supply of little birds and was devouring them with untold delight.

Startled by the display, the Entrusted Servant asked his companions if they knew who the remarkable character was.

"Name him anything you want and I will confirm it!" muttered Big Eye Clairy, from the corner of his mustache. "What name would be fitting for this strange monster?"

"To call him Bird Annihilator would sound reasonable. Or if we were to call him Stretch-Arms, it would suit him, too. Or Longneck, perhaps. But if we called him Birdy the Stretch, it would fit his odd ways," declared Entrusted Servant, deeply moved by the fate of the poor little birds.

"So be it, we will call him Birdy the Stretch. Now, what we know about him is that he is the son of the Archer and the Grandson of Sagittarius the Earth Belt and stairway to Heaven! He is also known to be the doom of every flying creature and the terror of all mankind! Fewer words would not do him justice," said Big Eye Clairy.

"Entrusted Servant, keep making fun of me, and my family!" said Birdy the Stretch. "But you would be smarter if you made fun of yourself! You have no idea what challenges are ahead of you. You may think that you can take hold of Emperor Red's daughter, but you haven't the slightest idea what a witch this young woman is! She can change herself into a magic bird at will. Once she has become a bird, try to catch her, if you can! Without a man of my abilities next to you, do not bother to exhaust your legs by going any further."

The Entrusted Servant looked at him again and said, "Join us! But please do us a favor. Every now and then, grab Frosty by his overcoat and carry him close to the sun, to warm him up a little. It will quiet his chattering teeth and cold breath. I feel cold chills in my back every time I look at him!"

Birdy the Stretch agreed to accompany Entrusted Servant and all six left together. The strange company caused a ruckus everywhere they went. Frosty set forests on fire, Hungry ate clay and dirt, seasoned with sand, ever yelling that he was starving, Thirsty emptied all the water from ponds and lakes, leaving the fish in agony without water, and the water snakes weakened so much that they were croaking like frogs. The only thing he left behind him was land as dry as a desert.

Big Eye Clairy kept peering into the most hidden secret places and crying into the wind, astonishing his companions with his declarations, "This girl has brown hair, that girl is a blond, there is a deer", or some other things without any importance. His ramblings were such nonsense regarding the moon and falling stars, that children or other bystanders were quick with a ready laugh at his meandering thoughts.

As for Birdy the Stretch, he kept catching birds in flight and throwing them into his mouth whole. He did not leave any to return to their nests, not matter their size.

The only one in the company who did no harm was the Entrusted Servant. He disapproved, but had no choice but to tolerate his companions until he could accomplish the orders received from Beardless. The Entrusted Servant accepted his odd allies the way they were and spoke kindly to them. He depended on each of them in his dealings with Emperor Red who, according to reputation, was a rascal of diabolic malice, who treated men worse than stray dogs. He remembered the old saying, 'When you deal with a thief you must be equal to one and a half thieves.' It seemed that at least one of his companions would be a match for the deadly tricks of Emperor Red.

*   *   *

The Entrusted Servant and his companions managed to get this far, and they kept going even farther, until finally they arrived at the great empire of Emperor Red. They made their way straight for his castle. The ragtag band entered the courtyard one by one, in a straight line, with the Entrusted Servant at the head.

The Entrusted Servant came before Emperor Red and told him from what part of the world he had come, giving the name of his master. The Emperor listened and was quite shocked to see the fellows in rags beside him, who had the audacity to come to him and to ask for nothing less than the Imperial daughter! It made no difference in whose name they had come, even if he were the most powerful of all rulers in the world. However, he did not allow his revulsion to show on his face and refrained from giving them an answer. He simply invited them to spend the night with him inside the palace. It would allow him to think about the request, he said.

Then, the Emperor called for one of his trusted subjects, and ordered him to escort the Entrusted Servant's group, in secret, to a compound which looked like a small house made of brass. It was made to be heated from underneath until the floor and the entire structure would turn glowing white and the guests within would find their eternal sleep, sharing the fate of so many past contenders, none of whom looked as deplorable as the Entrusted Servant's lot.

Once the instructions were given, the evil-minded Emperor hurried to visit the brass compound and set fire to twenty-four bundles of logs kept inside a narrow enclosure below the ground floor. Then, the Emperor watched with a smile at the corner of his mouth as the compound turned glowing red, like charcoal. At that point, the Emperor invited his guests to enter the compound and rest for the night.

In the meantime, Frosty, smarter than any other, gathered his companions and guided them to a place out of sight. He then whispered close to their ears, "Listen to me, do not allow the Devil to give you the urge to enter the brass guest house ahead of me! You will not live long and every one of you will burn alive in no time at all! There is no other man as wicked as this emperor. He is famous for his supposed goodness as well as the boundless evil that lies beneath! He will get rid of you at the very moment you leave you're back exposed. As for his daughter, she was molded by the Devil, the mirror image of her father and even worse than him! She reminds me of the old saying, 'When the female goat jumps with one hoof in the air, the male jumps effortlessly, ten times as far.' But let me tell you, mates. This time, they will get what they deserve! I will put an end to this cruelty or I will see myself hanged!"

"I feel the way you do," said Hungry. "Emperor Red thinks he can master even the Devil! But this time, he will lose his claws!"

"And I," said Big Eye Clairy, "feel confident that in the end, the Emperor will give up his last shirt to get rid of us!"

"All that you say is true, but now we need to rest to prepare for the coming challenges. The Emperor's assistant is waiting for us! He has already set the table and lit the candles and the servants are there to attend to us. Sharpen your teeth for the dinner and follow me."

They finished eating and left the dining hall, acting lazy and in no hurry. Once in front of the brass compound, they stopped. Frosty went ahead of them and blew a gust of air from his lungs. He exhaled three times through his benevolent lips and instantly the compound became neither too hot, nor too cold. It was just right for a good night's rest. They went inside and blew out the candles.

The Emperor did not see Frosty cooling their quarters. Outside the door, the guests could hear him say, "Sleep well, my little visitors. Enjoy your wonderful beds and your eternal sleep! Tomorrow morning, all that will be left of you is ashes!"

With that, he left them in the care of their fate and went about his own business.

In the meantime, the Entrusted Servant and his companions knew better and were in good spirits. Now that they had warmed themselves up, they realized how tired they were and they stretched out on their beds, teasing each other and for a while unconcerned with the daughter of Emperor Red.

Frosty covered himself with blankets and pillows, but could not stop shaking with cold. "I cooled this compound for you!" he complained. "Before I did that, it was just right for me! This is what happens when you are in the company of weaklings! Look at that fellow on my side, how cozy he is, while I am freezing to death! I will teach all of you fellows a lesson! I will shake so violently, that you won't be able to sleep, either!"

"Hush, Frosty!" said the others. "We will soon see the daylight and you keep on pestering us! If anyone would want your companionship, he should look exactly like you, the way two drops of water look identical. You will not allow us one single moment of rest with your endless grumbling and you grow angry for no reason at all! You are not made to live among decent folks or in some palace. You belong in the woods, surrounded by wolves and bears!"

"Now, just a moment!" protested Frosty. "Who do you think I am? Am I your humble servant? Don't you dare to change a deer into a donkey, it won't work with me! I am a good and decent man and that is a fact! But if you make me lose my patience, believe me, my modest protests will change to match the coachman I'm facing!"

"Listen to me, big mouth! When you get mad, you bleed from your eyes," yelled Hungry. "If I could, I would hide you behind a baker's shelf where he stocks his bread, but I am afraid it will not be large enough to hide your ears! And then, should you want to calm down, listen to me carefully, bring your lips tight together and try to understand that you are not alone in this place!"

"Ah!" Frosty raged. "I get what I deserve, perhaps even less! May the one of you who will do for the others as much as I did be rewarded with the same words!"

"You are right, Frosty, about everything you did for us. But now you do us wrong," observed Big Eye Clairy. "With all this arguing, we will lose the night's sleep! When someone spoils your rest when you need it most, how do you respond? You are lucky to deal with decent people like us. Others would not be so tolerant!"

"If this goes on, I will lengthen my legs and pass through the walls of this room. Then I will grab the roof, and use it to cover my ears and head too!" said Birdy the Stretch, exasperated. "Can't you keep quiet, at this late hour? This whole thing will bring us bad luck! Tell me, Big Lips, is any of this my fault?"

"It is his fault alone," argued Big Eye-Clairy. "He is so lucky! I can tell you what he deserves!"

"Make a guitar out of his stomach," said Thirsty. "Better yet, turn his scalp into hatchet and his belly into a drum, and then use his spine in place of a drumstick! At least it will serve a purpose! Otherwise, there will be no end to this madness!"

Once Frosty saw that everybody had turned against him, he took the matter seriously and in no time he covered the walls of the room with three inches of thick frost. They all froze, down to the marrow.

"Good for you, my beloved companions! I am now entirely at your service! Anything that may please you, ask for it. You will be served at once!" said Frosty, laughing maniacally. "How could I refrain from shaking with laughter when I look at you! I do not complain about the Entrusted Servant, who is completely decent! But you bullies, you act as if you never slept outside in the fields, where you had no beds! You pretend to be sons of unusual upbringing, who are used to resting on silk and gold sofas."

"Go on, Big Lips," replied the companions. "May you go on to your demise, together with all your ancestors, for the rest of eternity. Now, let us sleep and let us remain friends and when we will get up, let us help the Entrusted Servant! Anger and despair do not lead to paradise!"

Until sunrise, they continued to grumble and bicker and did not get much rest. With the return of daylight, the wicked Emperor Red, convinced it was all over with his strange guests, came down to inspect the guest compound and order that their ashes be swept away.

As he approached, he could not believe his eyes. The compound was covered with a thick layer of ice! It was impossible to see the doors and windows. From within came screams and a great clamor, with voices yelling, "What kind of Emperor is this? He lets us freeze and does not care! We were not offered even a wood log from the cellar! Even the most modest families would keep their homes heated with a fire! How undignified! Even the tongues in our mouths are frozen!"

Having heard all this, the Emperor Red was both frightened and furious. He went to the door and attempted to open it, but it was useless. He tried to break in but failed again. He went back to his quarters and brought along a number of workers with icepicks and large pots filled with boiling water. Some chopped the ice and others splashed the hot water over the door hinges and until they managed to open the door and bring the guests out. But then, what a sight! Their hair and beards were covered with icicles.

It was almost impossible to tell if they were men or phantoms.

As for Frosty, he was the most spectacular of them, with his prodigious shaking. His lips had such contortions that Emperor Red turned pale with dismay.

While this scene was unfolding, the Entrusted Servant came out of the compound to meet Emperor Red. He asked the Emperor, most courteously, "Most esteemed Majesty, allow me to repeat the purpose of my presence here. The mighty Emperor Green's nephew is anxiously waiting for me to come back and bring along your gracious daughter to become his bride! I hope that you would trust her in my care, so that your daughter and our delegation may leave in peace and return to our normal lives."

"Well, brave fellow," replied Emperor Red, "you must show some patience! All goes well for he who is capable of waiting! Let me offer you a light meal. I would hate to let you leave without food."

"Praise the Lord, Your Majesty! God speaks through your lips! My guts yell from hunger pangs!" replied Hungry.

"Perhaps Your Majesty will provide some moisture to our throats, since everything around us is so completely dry!" added Thirsty.

"Keep your mouths shut, don't say another word! His Majesty knows better what we need," argued Big Eye Clairy, whose eyelid kept fluttering open and shut.

"I am sure everything will be perfect," chimed Birdy the Stretch. "We are the guests of an Emperor! His Majesty will make sure that we will not be ignored and allowed to die from freezing, hunger or thirst!"

"Have you not heard that His Majesty is the father of all hungry and thirsty people?" said Frosty, still shaking with every muscle of his body. "I, for one, rejoice in thinking how warm I will get after I start drinking some wine!"

"Can't you quiet down?" snapped Hungry. "Stop harassing His Majesty with your endless blather! His Majesty knows what to order!"

"In my case," said Thirsty, "eating means nothing! Drinking is the only thing that counts! Since His Majesty intends to offer us a meal, it may be best if he fills us with drinks before we start eating, since drinks give us strength and energy! As they say, 'If you drink like a hero, you shall never feel you are not one!' I am only afraid that His Majesty may get confused and unable to figure out how to handle our expectations!"

"Let His Majesty offer us what he pleases, but I pray he will order everything right away," commented Hungry. "I am starving!"

"Have patience!" said Big Eye Clairy. "You are not sheltering starving mice inside your stomach!"

"You will be getting the beverages very shortly and the food, too," said the Emperor, "But you must eat and drink everything, for I do not tolerate waste!"

"May God always favor us with such offers, Your Highness," answered Hungry, while caressing his belly.

Thirsty jumped in to say, "And may God enlighten Your Majesty's mind to also bless us, not only with good meat, but with all the drinks that should go with it!" His mouth watered with anticipation.

The Emperor kept silent. He listened to them entirely disgusted, hiding his rage and thought. "Good God, let the Devil loose for just one moment and I will see how the Devil will chew me up! It will be you, Almighty God, who will pay for their wrong-doings!" The Emperor left the guests at the table and returned to the palace.

Shortly after he left, the guests received twelve carriages full with bread, twelve beautifully roasted oxen and twelve large barrels full of wine. The wine was so strong, it took only one sip to make a man stumble on his feet. It would go straight to his head, get the tongue sticky and loose at the same time to the point that one would start chatting in a forgotten ancient Turkish language.

After the food supplies were placed on the table, Hungry and Thirsty gave a brief speech.

"Dear companions, go ahead, eat and drink to your pleasure, but without overdoing it, or else you will get in trouble with us!"

The Entrusted Servant, Frosty, Big Eye Clairy and Birdy the Stretch went ahead and ate all they could and drank plenty. When they finished, it was impossible to tell how much they had, considering the bounty that had been brought to the table.

"Now, get out of our way, for you do nothing more than waste food and drink!" lamented Hungry and Thirsty in one voice and with that they lost their patience completely, tortured with cramps from hunger and thirst.

Hungry started helping himself to a carriage full of bread, which he swallowed in one motion. He added to it a whole roasted calf. After that, he went on eating the next and the next and so on until nothing was left on the table.

At the same time, Thirsty pierced the barrels with his teeth and sucked the wine in big, long gulps. As soon as he finished with one, he would immediately grab the next. He did not stop until each barrel was completely empty and did not spill a single drop of wine on the floor.

As soon as they finished, Hungry began yelling loudly again, complaining that he was starving and had horrible hunger pangs. He went as far as throwing the bones left on the table in the faces of the waiters while the Emperor was watching the scene, mouth open and stupefied.

Thirsty kept screaming from the top of his lungs that he was dying from thirst. He too, became irrational and began throwing barrels blindly, not caring where they landed.

In midst of all the chaos, the Emperor turned red with rage.

"This is unreal! God must have sent me these visitors to ruin me! Who can I turn to for counsel in this madness?"

The Entrusted Servant saw his chance, and stepping in front of the other companions, said, "Allow me to wish Your Majesty a long life! I hope that now I will be trusted with the Princess, your daughter, so that we leave in peace and accomplish our mission. Emperor Green's nephew must be anxious to see us back!"

"You are eager and hasty, my brave young man," replied the Emperor. "Have some more patience! My daughter does not run down the roads so that she can be picked up by some horse-riding traveler! Each one of you ate and drank as much as thirty people put together, and this I agreed to. But now, in return, you must work for me a little. I have the poppy seeds collected from twenty bushels, but they are mixed with sand. I will give you until tomorrow morning to separate each seed from the grains of sand. And I will not tolerate one single seed in the sand, nor a grain of sand mixed with the poppy seeds! If you succeed, I will remember it while I consider your request. If you fail, you will pay with your heads for your impudence. Your punishment will serve as an example to all those who expect more than they deserve!"

With that, the Emperor turned on his heel, sure that they would fail and he would finally be rid of them. The Entrusted Servant and his companions stared at each other helplessly.

"What a curse!" shouted Big Eye Clairy. "What a waste of time! What an evil mind this Emperor has! I can see quite well the poppy seeds and grains of sand, even in darkness, but how are we to separate each from the other? Only ants could do such a thing, and it would have to be a great deal of them, at that! It seems that the old saying is true. Never leave your fate in the hands of a redhead! The Devil may have conceived them in his own image, just like this emperor we must satisfy."

Suddenly, Entrusted Servant recalled the ant's wing and the promise that it stood for. He found it and set it afire. Then from everywhere ants appeared in a great mass. There were as many as the ashes in a bonfire or specks of dust on a road--even as many as the grass in the fields and the leaves of trees in a forest! The ants came by every path. Some of the ants fell from trees, down to the ground and it looked like the swarm would never end.

Immediately, they set themselves to the task. In no time at all, they separated the grains of sand and the poppy seeds and put them into two mounds. One could bet a fortune and still be unable to find one single grain of sand lost with the seeds, or a poppy seed lost in the sand.

At sunset, when sleep is sweet, and even Mother Earth slumbers, a number of ants entered the palace and viciously bit Emperor Red as he slept. Having felt the itches and burns, the Emperor jumped right out of his bed and could not fall back to sleep. He tossed and turned until noon.

Finally, he got up and he checked his bed with care, but the ants had vanished without a trace.

"Hell on earth!" he cried. "What are these red marks swelling all over my body? I see no reason!"

When the Emperor went to see the Entrusted Servant and his companions, he saw that his task had been completed. Rage boiled in his stomach. The Entrusted Servant found him there, lost in his thoughts. He repeated once more, after bowing with deference to the Emperor.

"Very esteemed Majesty, I hope that now you will entrust the Princess to us. All we want is to leave you in peace, as we came, and to return home."

"We will find time for all matters, brave young man," replied Emperor Red, with his voice trembling with anger. "Your work is not done yet! There is another thing you must do. I want you to guard my daughter's bedroom tonight. She sleeps there, as she always does! If she is still there tomorrow morning, I may consider giving her to you. However, if she is not there, I will be done with you, once and for all! Do you understand?"

"Quite well, great Emperor," said the Entrusted Servant. "I trust there will be no further conditions! I am concerned about my master, who keeps waiting for me. He may lose his patience!"

"What your master has in store for you is no concern of mine!" barked Emperor Red. "Should he decide to skin you, it would mean nothing to me. Watch over my daughter most carefully. Do it as if you were protecting your own eyes. If you fail, your life will be forfeit."

Once again the Emperor left them alone and went his way.

"The Devil must have taken part in this," said Frosty, shaking his head.

"I think he must be an old Devil, born from an even older mother. He is a concealed arrow at nighttime, turning into a demon, in plain daylight! But he will not gratify himself much longer with these insane tasks, let me tell you that!" Big Eye Clairy added.

At last, evening came again, for better or worse. The young girl went to her bedroom to sleep, as usual. The Entrusted Servant followed her to the door, where he remained to serve as her guard. The other companions guarded the distance between her door and entrance of the palace.

Midnight was getting close. A little before that hour, the Princess transformed herself into a bird. She flew up in the air, unnoticed by five of the companions who stood guard. However, when she passed next to Big Eye Clairy, he saw and warned Birdy the Stretch.

"We are about to lose the Princess! She just flew away and outside the castle. She is the Devil in the flesh, this little one! She tricked us, by shrinking into a small bird and is flying straight and fast like an arrow right under our noses. Keep silent and we will look out for her! I can find where she is hiding, but you must be able to catch her with your strange talent. After that, twist her neck a little, to tame her!"

They left the palace immediately. On the way out, Big Eye Clairy whispered to Birdy the Stretch, "I have already discovered her. She hides on the other side of the earth, lying flat on the ground underneath that bush! Go ahead stretch yourself, grab her and don't let go!"

Birdy the Stretch reached out his right hand, searching through the tall, wild grass on the opposite side of the earth, until he touched her feathers. But the bird slipped through his fingers and flew away to the top of a mountain, where she hid behind a rock.

'There she is!" Big Eye Clairy said again.

Once more, Birdy the Stretch elongated his body and searched behind the rocks, but the instant he was about to set his hands on the bird, it darted all the way to the moon and hid behind it.

"The bird is now hiding behind the moon!" Big Eye Clairy urged.

"If I catch this bird, I will teach her the lesson of her life!" Birdy the Stretch growled.

Once again, Birdy the Stretch reached and reached until he touched the moon. Then he grabbed the moon in his arms and picked the bird up by the tail. He was about to twist her neck when the bird reclaimed the shape of the young princess and screamed at him.

"Birdy the Stretch, do not take my life! I will return with you! I give you my word of honor, and swear on the Holy Seal of Oaths and on the grace of my father, and the most precious belongings we have!"

"You just go on talking! What favors and gifts would you have given us, had I not been able to see you sneaking out as a bird, you wicked witch!" replied, Birdy the Stretch. "You had us hunting you for a good quarter of an hour! Now, go back to bed, and hurry! It will be sunrise very shortly. As for what will happen from now on, we will find out soon."

They seized her, each holding one of her arms, and headed for the palace. It was sunrise when they walked in front of the guards. They forced her back into her bedroom.

"Now you see, Entrusted Servant, if we were not here, what would you have done?" they said. "I hope you now see that every human being has both good and bad within him! If the good prevails, the bad becomes unimportant. Without us, you would have had a long and pleasant sleep, but in the end we all would have faced death!"

The Entrusted Servant and the other companions were unable to reply. They lowered their heads with humility. The two who saved them from the wrath of Emperor Red were real heroes, and most of all, they showed what it meant to act like real brothers in hard times.

Then, down the hall came Emperor Red, excited, as if he was made of licking flames. He threw open the bedroom door. Against all expectations, he found his daughter sitting inside. He was speechless with fury.

"Most Gracious Majesty, I dare to hope that, finally, I will be trusted with your daughter, and that we will be able to leave in peace and resume our duties," said the Entrusted Servant.

"I told you to have patience, brave young man," said the Emperor darkly. "Everything in its due time! I did not tell you that I have another daughter, whom I have adopted. She has the same age, and looks exactly like my blood daughter, as if they were two drops of water. They are alike in every way namely beauty, waistline and the way they walk! Everything! Come with me! If you can identify my real blood daughter, you may take her with you and go home! Your presence has turned my hair white! I will go right now to get my daughters ready. If you guess right, so much the better for you! If you fail, take your belongings and do me the pleasure of leaving at once! I have had more than I can take with all of you!"

The Emperor made sure the princesses had the same hair and dress and then ordered the Entrusted Servant to come and determine which one was his daughter by blood.

The Entrusted Servant was confused and felt despair for he was so very close to completing his task yet did not know what to do. Then, he remembered the wing given to him by the Queen of the Bees. He took out the wing, set it to fire and instantly, the Queen of the Bees showed up next to him.

"Do you need me, Entrusted Servant?" she asked, while she rested on his shoulder. "I am here to help you!"

The Entrusted Servant hurried to tell the dire situation before him, and begged her from the bottom of his heart to find a way to help him.

"Do not worry, Entrusted Servant. Leave it to me to recognize her. She can be accompanied by another thousand who will look exactly like her, it doesn't matter! Just go and be brave! I will be there, too. As soon as you enter the room, stop for a moment and take a look at the two girls. Notice the one who will try to protect herself with her handkerchief when I fly their way. That one will be the daughter of the Emperor!"

The Entrusted Servant entered the room. The bee remained on his shoulder while he stood before Emperor Red and his two daughters, who looked strikingly alike.

For a while, he kept examining one daughter, then the other. Long moments passed while he remained there motionless. Then, suddenly, the Queen of the Bees flew directly at them and sat straight on the cheek of Emperor Red's daughter. She jumped, started screaming and protected herself with her handkerchief.

The Entrusted Servant did not hesitate for another second. He went straight for her and gently took her by the hand, saying to the Emperor, "Most esteemed Majesty, I trust you have no other reasons to oppose my respectful request to you, since I accomplished everything you ordered me to do!"

"I have no further requests of you, Entrusted Servant. Take her with you! Given that she was unable to outsmart you, this is your chance to prove yourself. You can control her! Brave young man, I trust her in your hands, all in good faith!" the Emperor responded.

"We must leave at once. My master may be an old man by now, so much time have we wasted," said the Entrusted Servant.

"Now, just a minute, my impatient, dear sir!" protested the Princess. She grabbed in her hands a turtledove and whispered something into its ear, while kissing the bird affectionately. "Don't be in such a rush, Entrusted Servant. You may still fail in your mission! I too, have a right to say something! Before we leave, your horse and my turtledove must supply me with the Water of Life and also the Water of Death. They must also bring me three twigs from the Sweet Apple Tree. They will be found at the very spot where there are two mountains clashing against each other. Now, if my turtledove gets there first and brings me the water and the twigs, do not expect me to go. I will not follow you, no matter what! However, if by some chance, your horse gets back first and brings me what I requested, I promise to follow you wherever you go!"

The turtledove and the horse departed without delay. They raced, one on ground, the other in the air, trying their best to get ahead of each other. The turtledove, being lighter, arrived there first. She watched carefully the moment when the sun was about to set, when both mountains would take a rest.

At that split second, the turtledove plunged through the volcanic ashes, picked three twigs from the Sweet Apple Tree. Then she sped off to retrieve the Water of Life and the Water of Death. With everything the Princess required, the turtledove made her way back. When she reached the two mountains again, she saw the horse coming her way.

The horse asked her to stop for just a moment, and flattered the bird in every way conceivable, saying, "Turtledove, oh, my very beautiful little bird, do me the favor of letting me have your three twigs of Sweet Apple Tree and also the Water of Life, together with the Water of Death. You could return and get another supply! It will be easy for you to catch up with me, since you are so much lighter! Please, don't think too much about it! Let me have them and I assure you it will bring salvation and happiness to both my master and your princess and to both of us, who want them happy! If you don't want to do that, the Entrusted Servant will face death and all of us will be doomed to die!"

The turtledove listened and pondered. That was all the horse needed. He jumped into the air, grabbed the water and the twigs and ran back to the palace of Emperor Red. He gave the Princess the invaluable goods she requested. The Entrusted Servant was watching the scene and his heart was overcome with joy for the first time in a long time.

The turtledove showed up almost immediately after, but it was too late. The Princess looked at the bird and said to her. "Bird of mine, the only thing you can do now is to fly ahead of us and inform Emperor Green that we are coming." The turtledove took to the air at once.

The Princess knelt down at the feet of her father and said, "Please, dear father, grant me your blessings and may God keep you in good health! This is my destiny and I will learn to accept it! I must follow the Entrusted Servant. There is nothing more to say!"

After saying goodbye to her father, the Princess took along all the things she needed for the long journey ahead and mounted the saddle of a magic horse. The Entrusted Servant gathered his companions and they took off together.

*   *   *

On the return journey, Frosty, Hungry, Thirsty, Birdy the Stretch and also the delightful Big Eye Clairy said their sad goodbyes one by one. They asked to be forgiven for their shortcomings, for even those who seem bad can still see good prevail within. The Entrusted Servant thanked every one of them.

The Princess smiled as she watched the Entrusted Servant. In the evening, when the moon vanished from the sky, an arrow sparkled out of nowhere, crossed through their hearts, leaving behind it love, beautiful and burning hot like the shining sun. More and more, as they rode or walked together, the Entrusted Servant was enthralled by her beauty.

Finally, they arrived at the castle of Emperor Green. The Entrusted Servant had no idea what awaited him there. The turtledove had reached the castle ahead of them, telling the Emperor to expect the return of the Entrusted

Servant, who had accomplished his mission and brought back the Princess.

As soon as the Emperor got word, he prepared for their arrival. When the Entrusted Servant and the Princess approached the palace, they were announced by the herald and Emperor Green, his daughters, Beardless and the entire court, came out to meet them.

Beardless was stunned to see how beautiful the daughter of Emperor Red was, and rushed to assist her in dismounting her horse, trying to catch her in his arms. But the Princess resisted and pushed him aside with revulsion.

"Get out of my way, Beardless! I did not come here for you! I came here for Entrusted Servant! He, and only he, is the blood nephew of Emperor Green!"

Hearing such a statement, Emperor Green and his daughters turned mute with shock. They remained there motionless, like statues. Beardless, when he understood that his mask was gone, jumped like a mad dog on top of the Entrusted Servant, who fell down to the ground. With one stroke from his sword, Beardless cut his throat, yelling, "This is what you deserve, since you broke your oath of allegiance to me!"

But the Entrusted Servant had never said a word. At that moment, the Entrusted Servant's horse reared and came down to crush Beardless

"Enough with you, Beardless!" the horse shouted and took the evil man's head between his teeth where he crushed it and turned it to dust.

The Princess, daughter of Emperor Red, rushed to the Entrusted Servant and held his head on his shoulders, placing around him the three twigs of Sweet Apple Tree. She poured the Water of Death over his neck wound to stop the bleeding and when the skin healed together, she splashed over him the Water of Life. As soon as it fell upon him, the Entrusted Servant breathed and was alive once again! He wiped his eyes with the back of his hands, sighed, and whispered, "I fell in such a deep sleep!"

"You would have slept for a very long time, had I not been here," replied Emperor Red's daughter, the lovely Princess, while she kissed him tenderly. Then she gave him back his sword.

Right then, they knew that they belonged together. They went in front of Emperor Green, knelt at his feet and asked for his blessing and swore fidelity to each other. There, the Emperor granted them his empire.

The joyful wedding ceremony was quick to follow, drawing people from around the world. Even the sky, sun and moon could not stop smiling upon them. Many who had helped them in their arduous quests came to celebrate. Amongst them came the Queen of the Ants, the Queen of the Bees and the Queen of the Fairies, the most gracious and miraculous Holy Mother Sunday. They also invited beautiful queens and great kings and someone else too: a modest storyteller, counting his days one by one, before he too will fall into complete oblivion.

All guests were caught up in joy, drinking and dancing. Even the poorest among beggars joined them. The happy event lasted for years! It goes on still! Whoever comes this way will be able to eat and drink all that they can manage!

In the meantime, as for ourselves and our own lives those of us who are productive, can eat and drink as we please, while the ones who do not want to do anything can only watch the others and tighten their belts!

THE END